Wishes really do come true

Lucky Stars

Lucky Star that shines so bright,
Who will need your help tonight?
Light up the sky, it's thanks to you
Wishes really do come true . . .

Lucky Stars

The Best Friend Wish

The Perfect Pony Wish

The Pop Singer Wish

The Birthday Wish

The Film Star Wish

The Ballerina Wish

Explore the sparkling world of the stars at

www.luckystarsbooks.co.uk

Wishes really do come true

Lucky Stars

The Film Star Wish

Phoebe Bright

Illustrated by Karen Donnelly

MACMILLAN CHILDREN'S BOOKS

Special thanks to Valerie Wilding

First published 2012 by Macmillan Children's Books
a division of Macmillan Publishers Limited
20 New Wharf Road, London N1 9RR
Basingstoke and Oxford
Associated companies throughout the world
www.panmacmillan.com

ISBN 978-1-4472-0251-6

1 3 5 7 9 8 6 4 2

A CIP catalogue record for this book is available from
the British Library.

Printed and bound by CPI Group (UK) Ltd, Croydon CR0 4YY

For Zack Littley

Contents

Hello, friend!

I'm Stella Starkeeper and I want to tell you a secret. Have you ever gazed up at the stars and thought how magical they looked? Well, you're right. Stars really do have magic!

Their precious glittering light allows me to fly down from the sky, all the way to Earth. You see, I'm always on the lookout for boys and girls who are especially kind and helpful. I train them to become Lucky Stars - people who can make wishes come true!

So the next time you're under the twinkling night sky, look out for me. I'll be floating among the stars somewhere. Do give me a wave!

Love from
Stella x

1
Strawberries and Sparkles

Cassie Cafferty was the only early-morning customer at Farmer Greg's 'pick your own' fruit farm. Hundreds of ripe red strawberries still dotted the lush green plants, but her basket was full.

Cassie picked one last giant berry and popped it in her mouth. So juicy!

At the checkout, Farmer Greg said cheerily, 'Hello, young Cassie. Goodness, you've got enough strawberries here for everyone in Astral-on-Sea!'

'Mum's making
strawberry meringues as
a treat for the guests at
Starwatcher Towers,'
said Cassie.

'It's a busy life,
running a bed and
breakfast, I'm
sure,' said
Farmer
Greg.

'You're right,' said Cassie. She paid and
took her basket. The scent from the sun-
warmed fruit was sweet. 'Mmmm!' she said.
'The guests will love these. Bye!'

Cassie headed along the edge of Whimsy

Wood. There were a few dog-walkers
about, but otherwise she had the path to
herself. She swung her basket as she went,
being careful not to lose any strawberries.

Something in the wood caught Cassie's
eye. She peered among the trees. Sunlight
dappled the leaves but, further in among the
shadows, there was . . . yes! It was an orb of
silver light, like a fallen star.

Cassie smiled. *Could that light be Stella
Starkeeper?* she wondered. She hoped it was!

As Cassie pulled a branch aside, the
charms on her silver bracelet tinkled. Stella
Starkeeper had given her the bracelet on
her seventh birthday, a few weeks ago. It
held a magical secret!

Each charm gave Cassie a special power.

Lucky Stars

Whenever she helped make someone's wish come true, she received a new charm. Once she received seven charms, she would become a Lucky Star. So far she had five. The little bird gave her the power to fly, and the crescent moon helped her to talk to animals. With the silver butterfly she could stop time, and with the flower charm she could make things appear.

Cassie's newest charm was a cute cupcake, but she and her friend, Alex, still hadn't discovered its power. Alex

was the only other person who knew about the magical charms – apart from Stella, of course. Alex was staying at Starwatcher Towers for a couple of weeks with his parents and his puppy, Comet. He and Cassie had become firm friends.

Cassie watched the silver light dance further into the trees.

'It's going!' she gasped. 'I must see if it really is Stella!' She chased the light, but it moved too swiftly.

Cassie realized she needed the bracelet's magical power if she was to catch it up. She concentrated hard on her bird charm. Her wrist tingled. Sparkles swirled from the bracelet, then spiralled around her.

Cassie rose off the ground and flew after

the light. She moved quickly through the trees, clutching her basket carefully so it wouldn't get caught on a branch.

The light continued along the deserted

main path through Whimsy Wood, straight towards Astral-on-Sea's open-air cinema.

In a few moments, Cassie reached the clearing. A giant screen was set up. There were rows of benches on which to sit, and a large grassy area where families could have a picnic. During film screenings, refreshments were sold at the kiosk that stood to one side.

Cassie spotted the silver light twinkling in front of a poster. There

11

was a film showing that afternoon.

That sounds interesting, thought Cassie as she drifted gently to the ground.

Suddenly the light burst into thousands of tiny sparkles that swirled towards her. Then, with a *shoosh* and a *whoosh* and a *whizz-fizz-fizz,* the sparkles gathered into a dazzling column of light.

Cassie's heart skipped a beat as the light changed into a lovely young woman with long fair hair. She held a wand, tipped with a twinkling star, and all her clothes were silver. She wore glittery leggings and glossy boots beneath a silky dress that rippled in the breeze. Star-shaped buttons glittered on the cuffs of her shiny cropped jacket, and she wore a glistening crown, woven from the finest silver strands.

The woman smiled and her velvety-blue eyes twinkled.

'Hello, Stella!' cried Cassie, running to hug her.

'What a lovely welcome,' Stella said in her soft, warm voice. 'And what wonderful strawberries.'

'Try them!' said Cassie.

Stella took one. 'It's heart-shaped!' she said. Then she tasted it. 'Mmm, so sweet!' She touched Cassie's bracelet with her wand. 'You have earned five charms already.'

Cassie nodded. 'If I earn two more,' she said, 'I'll become a true Lucky Star, like you.'

The Film Star Wish

'Yes, and then you can grant any wish you like, as long as you feel it's right. But until then you must listen carefully to my clues and to hear the right wish.' She smiled. 'Do you like your new cupcake charm?'

'It's lovely,' said Cassie, 'but I don't know what power it has. Can you tell me?' she asked. 'Or maybe give me a clue?'

Stella raised her wand above Cassie. Brilliant light shone down from it to form a shining pool.

Cassie felt as if she was standing in a spotlight. She twirled like a ballerina. 'Do I look like a star onstage?' she asked, laughing.

Stella smiled. 'Not everybody enjoys being in the spotlight, Cassie.'

She
popped
another
heart-shaped
strawberry
into her
mouth.
Then,
with a
wave
of her wand, she
vanished behind
a veil of silvery
sparkles.

As the sparkles drifted away, Cassie
turned towards home, thinking over what
Stella had said.

'*Not everybody enjoys being in the
spotlight . . .*'

Was it a clue? If so, whatever could it
mean?

2
Roxy Gold!

Cassie came out of Whimsy Wood on to the road that went through Astral-on-Sea and along by the beach. She glanced up at Starwatcher Towers, her cliff-top home, where she imagined Mum busy baking meringues to go with the strawberries. She thought Dad might be in his observatory. He was an astronomer, and he was probably making notes about the stars he saw through his telescopes at night.

Lucky Stars

The sun
glinted off
the glass
roof of Cassie's own
cosy bedroom. She
often lay on her bed
and watched the stars
through it. She giggled
to herself. Dad didn't know that she could
also float up through an open panel in the
roof and fly among the stars with Stella!

Suddenly, Cassie heard a familiar noise.
'Hee-haw-hee-haw-hee-haw!'

Bert's donkeys! But they should be on
the beach, giving rides to children.

Cassie hurried round the bend and
there was Bert with three donkeys –

in the middle of the road!

'Move, you daft animals,' Bert was saying. 'You're blocking the way.'

Cassie giggled. Those donkeys could be difficult! 'I'll help,' she cried.

Lucky Stars

Bert wiped his forehead. 'Thanks, Cassie,' he said. 'A speedboat came too near the beach, and Coco ran off in fright. Of course, the others followed.' He tried to push a donkey out of the road, but the stubborn animal wouldn't move. 'Lucky no one was riding them at the time.'

'And lucky there are no cars around,' said Cassie. She patted her favourite donkey. 'Poor Coco, you're so timid. No wonder

the speedboat frightened you.' She held out a fat strawberry. 'Here, would you like this?'

As Coco tried to nibble it, Cassie walked backwards to the pavement. Coco followed, stretching for the strawberry. He was just about to step out of the road, when a car came round the bend and glided to a stop.

Coco trotted back to his friends.

'Oh no!' groaned Bert, looking even more hot and flustered.

Cassie felt sorry for him. 'Don't worry,' she said. 'I'll explain to the driver. I'm sure he won't mind waiting a few minutes.'

The car was creamy white, with black windows, and it was very long.

Wow! A stretch limo, thought Cassie. *I wonder who's inside.*

The rear window behind him opened, and a pretty girl looked out. She was a little

older than Cassie, and wore a scarlet top
with sequined hearts on it, skinny jeans,
high-heeled boots and a red-and-gold
necklace. Her glossy black hair tumbled
over her shoulders as she leaned forward,
holding a pen and a photograph.

Cassie recognized her instantly. She was
the famous movie star, Roxy Gold! Cassie
opened her mouth to speak, but she was so
surprised that no words came out. What on
earth was Roxy Gold doing in Astral-on-
Sea?

Roxy gazed dreamily at the beach for a
moment. Then she looked at Cassie and
flashed her famous smile.

'Who shall I write it to?' asked Roxy.

Cassie realized that Roxy thought

25

she wanted an autograph and felt herself blushing. 'Oh, er, no . . .' she said. 'I mean, yes, please, but . . . I really just wanted to explain about the donkeys.'

'Donkeys?' said Roxy, leaning further out to see. 'Oh, aren't they sweet. I'll come and help!'

'That would be great,' Cassie cried. 'Thank you!'

Roxy opened the door. 'Pete,' she said to the driver, 'can you wait here, please?'

Pete grinned. 'Those donkeys aren't letting me go anywhere!'

Roxy laughed.

'I'll show you Coco,' said Cassie. 'He's my favourite.'

They all tried to coax the donkeys out of the road. But clicking tongues, patting and stroking made no difference to the stubborn creatures.

A small crowd had started to gather on the beach, staring at the limo. A little boy gave a gasp. 'Mum!' he shouted. 'That's Roxy Gold!'

Cassie felt quite important. Fancy people

seeing her, Cassie Cafferty, chatting to a movie star!

She wondered if anyone she knew was watching. To her delight, behind two wildly waving girls, she spotted a curly-haired boy with a fluffy white puppy and a big bag of library books.

'Hey! Alex!' she called to her friend.

He was hopping about with excitement, pointing at Roxy.

Cassie beckoned to him.

Alex's eyes widened. He slipped through the crowd and dropped his book bag on the pavement's edge.

28

'Sit, Comet,' he said.

The puppy leaned against Cassie, wagging his tail madly.

Roxy was busy signing autographs.

'Excuse me, Roxy,' said Cassie, 'this is my friend, Alex. He's going to be a scientist.'

'Hi, Alex,' said Roxy. Then she noticed Comet. 'Oh, you gorgeous ball of fluff!' she said, cuddling him. 'Alex, you're so lucky. I can't have a puppy because I travel so much.'

Alex went bright red. 'Hello, Roxy,' he said shyly. 'I – I saw you in *Space Girl*. You were brilliant. And – um – and in *Tessa's Time Machine*.'

'Thanks!' said Roxy. She looked so

thrilled that Alex grinned the widest grin
Cassie had ever seen!

*Roxy must be super-famous if Alex recognizes
her,* she thought. *He's usually too wrapped up
in his science experiments to pay much attention
to film stars.*

At last, the donkeys decided to go back to the beach.

But Roxy was still signing autographs, smiling brightly. Every now and then, she looked longingly at the car.

'She must be keen to get going,' Cassie murmured to Alex. 'I wonder if her hand hurts from signing so many autographs.'

Alex just stared. 'I can't believe Roxy Gold spoke to me,' he said. 'And to Comet too!'

Cassie smiled. 'She's going to speak to us again,' she whispered as Roxy walked towards them.

'We've heard about a lovely B & B near here,' said Roxy. 'If there's room, we'd like to stay there for a while.'

'It's called Starwatcher Towers,' added
Roxy's dad. 'Have you heard of it?'

Cassie and Alex grinned at each other,
and Cassie guessed they'd both had the
same exciting thought.

Roxy Gold's staying with us!

3
A Star at Starwatcher Towers

'Starwatcher Towers is my mum's B & B,' said Cassie.

'Fantastic!' said Roxy. 'Could you show us the way?'

Cassie nodded. 'Sure!'

Roxy opened the car door. 'Jump in,' she said. 'You too, Alex. And you, gorgeous,' she added to Comet, giving him a stroke.

Cassie sank into a scarlet leather seat next to Roxy, and held her strawberry basket on her knees. Alex sat beside Cassie, and Comet settled on the deep red carpet. Roxy's dad was sitting at the other end of the limo.

Pete the driver started the car. 'Which way?' he asked.

'Take the beach road through town, then up the hill to the cliff top,' said Cassie. She sat back and looked around the limo, at the pretty lights and mirrors. 'This is much more glamorous than getting around on a bike!' she said.

'I'd prefer to be riding a bike,' said Roxy. 'But the film company insist I use the limo. They want me to act like a star all the time. Anyway,' she added, 'I'm always so busy filming that I've never had time to learn how to ride a bike.'

'Really?' said Cassie. 'I'll teach you.'

'Fab, thanks!' said Roxy. She opened a small cupboard door. 'Fancy a drink?'

Cassie gasped. 'A fridge in a car!'

Roxy grinned. 'And it's full of lemonade,' she said. 'Want one?' She passed drinks to Alex and her dad, who were chatting about the car's dials and switches and buttons.

As they sipped their lemonade, Roxy opened the window. 'I love that sea smell,' she said.

Cassie giggled as Comet climbed on to Roxy's lap.

'He wants to sniff the sea too,' said Roxy. She helped him up so he could look out of the window. 'Ooh, look – the Fairy-cake Bakery!'

'My friend Kate lives there,' said Cassie. 'And there's the Pier Theatre, and Bert's candyfloss stall, and look – the fair's still here.' She stopped. 'It's not as exciting as places you're used to.'

'Astral-on-Sea looks great,' said Roxy,

smiling. 'I've already discovered it's a
friendly place.'

The car swung uphill. Cassie gripped her
basket of strawberries as Alex's bag of books
fell off the seat. He gathered it up and
pulled out a crumpled leaflet.

'What's that?'
asked Roxy.

Alex smoothed
it out. 'It's from
the library,' he
said. 'A film
about local
legends is being
shown this
afternoon.'

'I saw a poster about that,' said Cassie.

37

'It's at the open-air cinema in Whimsy Wood.'

'Whimsy Wood!' said Roxy. 'What a wonderful name.'

Alex went pink. Cassie thought he was about to speak, but she knew how shy Alex was. *He'll never ask her*, she thought. Aloud she said, 'Roxy, would you like to come to the open-air cinema with us?'

'I'd love to,' said Roxy with a smile. 'Thanks!'

As they reached Starwatcher Towers, Cassie's mum opened the front door. She watched Cassie climb out of the gleaming limo, followed by Alex, Comet and Mr Gold.

'What on earth . . . ?' Mrs Cafferty began in surprise, but she stopped as someone else emerged from the car.

Cassie laughed at
her mum's amazed
expression.

'You're Roxy
Gold!' said
Mrs Cafferty.
'Goodness! Are
you filming in
Astral-on-Sea?'

Mr Gold
shook her hand.

'I'm Roxy's dad,' he said. 'We're here for
a quiet holiday, but we haven't booked
anywhere. We wondered if . . .'

'Of course!' said Mrs Cafferty. 'I have
two nice rooms available. Come in!

Why not join us for lunch?'

Mr Gold followed her indoors, but Roxy stopped and looked up.

'What's that funny round room?' she asked Cassie.

'My bedroom,' Cassie said. 'Come and see.'

They ran upstairs, followed by Alex and Comet.

Roxy stared around the room. 'I love your starry wallpaper,' she said, 'and the moon-shaped lamp.' She looked up and gasped. 'Wow! A glass ceiling!'

They heard Mum's voice call, 'Lunch in five minutes!'

Quickly, Cassie showed Roxy to her guest room.

The Film Star Wish

'What a gorgeous view,' said Roxy. 'There's the beach and – look! Bert's donkeys too! Oh, Cassie, I love it here already.'

She opened her suitcase, and pulled out her wash-bag and a denim skirt. 'I must change into something comfy.'

'OK, see you downstairs,' said Cassie, turning to go.

'Mee-owwwww!'

Cassie looked back. Twinkle, her dear old cat, must have been hiding under the bed. Now he was turning round and round in Roxy's suitcase, settling down

on her purple silk pyjamas!

'Twinkle!' cried Cassie.

Roxy smiled. 'It's OK – leave him there,' she said. 'He looks so cosy. But why is he mewing so much?' She went into the bathroom, laughing. 'It's almost as if he's talking to you.'

He probably is, Cassie thought. She concentrated on her crescent-moon charm. Silvery sparkles danced around her bracelet and swirled between her and Twinkle. Cassie knew it was giving her the power to understand animals.

Twinkle blinked his amber eyes. 'She didn't throw me out,' he said. 'I like her, and I like it in this box thing.'

Cassie blew him a kiss, then called out,

'Roxy, Twinkle likes snuggling in your suitcase.'

'Tell him I'm really pleased that he likes it!' yelled Roxy.

Cassie whispered, 'Twinkle, Roxy's happy too.'

'Well, of course,' Twinkle purred. 'I'm enough to make anyone happy.'

The Film Star Wish

Roxy appeared, drying her face on a towel. She stroked Twinkle gently.

'Oh, Cassie,' she said. 'This is going to be the best holiday ever!'

4
An Accident

Cassie laid extra places for lunch. Pete
was joining them too, before
returning the limo to the studio.

After salad and crusty
bread, Mrs Cafferty fetched
the dish of strawberry
meringues and a blue
jug full of thick
yellow cream.

'Cassie picked the

strawberries this morning,' she said.

Cassie remembered giving some strawberries to Stella Starkeeper at the open-air cinema. That reminded her about Alex's leaflet.

'Mum,' she asked, 'can we go to see *Secrets of Astral-on-Sea* at the Whimsy Wood cinema this afternoon?'

'Of course,' said Mum. 'Just a moment.' She took an old book from the bookcase. 'This is called *Astral-on-Sea Mysteries*.' She showed everyone a picture of Whimsy Wood.

Roxy drew a sharp breath. 'There are

golden lights among the trees!'

'They're supposed to be the fairies of Whimsy Wood,' said Mrs Cafferty. 'When I was a girl, I used to hunt for them. I never saw one, though.'

'Nor me,' said Cassie. *But,* she thought, *I have seen a magical light among the trees!*

'The legend is well known,' Mum went on. 'I think secretly everyone would love to see a fairy.'

Just then some B & B guests came in. The young couple stared in surprise when they saw who was at the table. Mrs Cafferty fetched extra plates and said, 'We've lots of strawberry meringues left. Do have some!'

The guests said they'd eat their desserts in the garden. 'We won't intrude on Miss Gold,' said one.

When Pete left, Cassie's dad showed Mr Gold around his observatory. Alex helped Cassie clear up, while Roxy went into the garden to say hello to the guests.

'That's kind of her,' Cassie said. 'I expect they were dying to meet her.' Then she whispered, 'While we're out, I must listen for someone making a wish. If I make it come true, I'll earn another charm.'

Alex put the pepper pot away. 'I hope you do. I really want you to become a Lucky Star before my holiday's over.' Comet yipped and tilted his head to look up at Cassie with his big brown eyes. 'So does Comet,' Alex laughed.

Cassie felt sad. Alex had become such a

good friend
that she
couldn't
imagine him
not being
around any

more. She was going to miss him and
Comet so much when they had to leave.

'We must give Comet a walk before the
cinema,' said Alex.

'I know!' said Cassie. 'Let's invite Roxy
to come for a walk with us. We can go to
Whimsy Wood afterwards.'

Alex looked down. 'Can you ask?' he
said shyly. 'She's just coming up the path.'

'Course,' said Cassie. She opened the
kitchen door. 'Roxy, we're going to walk

Comet before the cinema. Want to come?'

'Love to!' she replied.

Ten minutes later, Cassie, Alex, Roxy
and Comet ambled down to the beach.
They waved to Bert with his line of
donkeys, and Cassie called hello to Bert's
son at the candyfloss stall.

At the pier, Roxy stopped. 'Look! An
ice-cream kiosk,' she said. 'I'll buy you
both an ice cream as a thank-you for being
so friendly.'

'You needn't thank us!' said Cassie.

Roxy hesitated for a moment. 'You do
like me, don't you? It's not just because I'm
a movie star?'

Cassie looked at Alex, then said, 'We
like you a lot! Not movie-star-Roxy, but

our new friend, Roxy. And we would
definitely like an ice cream!'

Roxy grinned. 'Will you go up and
get them, Cassie?' she asked. 'Here's the
money.'

Cassie looked at her, surprised.

The Film Star Wish

'I might be recognized,' Roxy explained, 'and it's so nice just being the three of us.'

'OK,' said Cassie.

While Cassie joined the queue for ice creams, Roxy waited with Alex and Comet. But Comet barked excitedly and the kiosk man looked across at them.

'Hey!' he said. 'You're Roxy Gold!' He called to the woman in the burger van. 'Look, Janice! It's Roxy Gold!'

Soon Roxy was surrounded by people taking photos with their mobiles and asking for autographs.

Cassie felt sorry for her. Fancy having all that fuss, when Roxy just wanted to be an ordinary girl. She moved to Roxy's side. 'Let's go to the high street,' she whispered.

'Then we'll head for Whimsy Wood.'

Alex carried Comet along the high street, in case he tripped people up on the narrow pavements. They passed the Fairy-cake Bakery and Cassie laughed when Kate's mum stared, open-mouthed, at Roxy!

The Film Star Wish

A little crowd had followed, and more people joined along the way, all so excited to see a famous film star.

Cassie showed Roxy the Flashley Manor Hotel, with its grand entrance and gold sign. 'It's run by the parents of a girl I know, Donna Fox,' she said. 'As Donna's always saying, it's the poshest hotel in town.'

Suddenly, Cassie stumbled as she was jostled from behind.

Roxy had a brave smile on her face, but the crowd was still growing.

A man with a large camera called, 'Smile, Roxy!'

Cassie desperately tried to think how to help. If she used the flying charm, everyone

would see. Talking to animals was no use. Maybe the cupcake charm could help – but how?

She stopped suddenly as Donna Fox appeared in front of her, scowling.

'Got a new friend?' Donna asked Cassie. 'Don't you know that movie stars are meant to stay at our hotel?'

Before Cassie could reply, a little girl ran

towards them, waving a pen and notebook.
But Roxy was signing an autograph and
didn't notice.

The girl tugged at Roxy's
sleeve. 'Please can I—' she
began.

But she pulled so
hard that Roxy
tripped, and her foot
slipped off the edge of
the pavement. Down
she fell, into the road.

'Ow!' she cried. 'My
knee!'

Quickly, Cassie and
Alex helped Roxy
to her feet.

Cassie was horrified. Her friend's leg was grazed and bleeding, and her face was white.

Poor Roxy!

5
Kara

'I'm sorry,' the little girl whispered.

Roxy patted her shoulder. 'It's OK – I'm fine,' she said gently, but Cassie could see that her eyes were swimming with tears.

I must find somewhere quiet, Cassie thought. She guided Roxy towards the nearest shop. Curtains covered the window and door, and a sign said, 'Grand opening tomorrow', but Cassie could hear someone moving inside. She knocked.

A woman with pink spiky hair opened the door. 'Whatever's wrong?' she asked.

'Please,' said Cassie, 'our friend needs to sit quietly for a moment. Can we come in?'

The Film Star Wish

'Of course,' said the woman. She ushered them inside and closed the door firmly. 'My name's Kara.'

Cassie moved aside a broom that hung from the ceiling. *It looks like a witch's broomstick*, she thought.

'I'm Cassie,' she said, 'and this is Alex, and this is . . .' Her voice trailed off. Roxy wouldn't want more fuss.

'Don't worry,' Kara said. 'I recognize you, of course, Roxy, but I promise peace and quiet while you're here.' She looked at Roxy's knee. 'And a plaster! I'll fetch one.'

'Thank you, Kara,' said Roxy. She managed a brave smile, then burst into tears.

Cassie shifted a heap of clothing from

a chair so Roxy could sit down. Kara
returned with her first-aid box and began to
clean the scraped knee.

'All I want is a quiet holiday,' Roxy
sobbed, 'but, wherever I go, people crowd
around. I can't be just me.'

Cassie hugged her, finding it hard to believe that a famous star was crying on her shoulder.

'Oh, Cassie,' Roxy sighed. 'I wish I could go about, unnoticed, just for one day . . .'

Cassie froze, then looked at Alex. His eyes were wide.

Roxy made a wish, she thought. *I have to help make it come true. But how?* She touched her new cupcake charm, thinking, *I must be able to use it somehow. But what power does it have?*

Just then, Comet jumped up next to Roxy, gazing at her with sympathy. On the chair beneath him Cassie noticed something that looked like a sparkly silver mermaid's tail.

A mermaid's tail? That's strange, she thought, looking around the shop for the first time.

Racks of clothes stood against the walls. There was a cowboy outfit, and a ballerina's tutu, a scarecrow costume and an astronaut's spacesuit. She glanced down at the clothes she'd moved from the chair.

'A Captain Hook outfit!' she said. 'And Peter Pan's hat . . . a giant rabbit . . .' She picked up something bright green and frizzy. 'A witch's wig!'

Kara smiled. 'I'm opening a fancy-dress shop,' she said. 'Costumes people will really notice!'

If Kara makes outfits people notice, Cassie

thought, *maybe I could find a costume that does the opposite – one that nobody notices at all.*

'Kara,' she said, 'please would you lend us some things? Just for the afternoon?'

Everyone looked puzzled.

'It's to help Roxy,' Cassie said.

'Of course,' said Kara.

Cassie found a pair of baggy trousers and a top decorated with palm trees. 'Roxy, put these on.'

'But . . .' Roxy began.

'If you wear a disguise, people won't recognize you,' Cassie explained. 'It'll be like you're invisible.'

Alex fished in a box. 'Try these too,' he said, passing Roxy some sunglasses. 'We met a singer called Jacey Day, and she used dark glasses when she didn't want to be recognized.'

Cassie swished the curtain across the doorway of the changing room. When Roxy reappeared, she did a twirl. 'How do I look?' she asked, adjusting the sunglasses.

'Just a sec!' said Cassie.

She hunted through a cardboard box and pulled out a baseball cap. She put it on Roxy's head and tucked

her long black hair inside so they couldn't
be seen.

'There!' Cassie said. 'Everyone will think
you're a tourist come to the seaside for the
day.'

Alex laughed. 'You look more like my
cousin Suzie than Roxy Gold, movie star!'

Kara clapped her hands. 'Amazing!' she
said. 'Look in the mirror.'

Roxy smiled when she saw her
reflection. 'That's brilliant!' she said. 'Thank
you, everyone. Let's try it out!'

Kara led them out of the back of the shop
and opened a door that led on to a side
street. 'All quiet,' she said.

Roxy hugged Kara and said, 'You've
been so kind.'

'We'll bring the clothes back tomorrow, Kara,' said Cassie. 'And we'd love to help with the Grand Opening – with Roxy in disguise, of course!'

Roxy held up crossed fingers. 'Let's hope this works!'

Cassie crossed her fingers too, wondering, *Will Roxy's disguise be enough to make her wish come true?*

6
Trouble in Whimsy Wood

As the friends drew near to Whimsy Wood, they joined groups of people, all heading along the woodland path towards the open-air cinema.

'No one's recognized you so far,' Cassie whispered.

'I know!' Roxy said happily, pushing the sunglasses further up the bridge of her nose.

Just before the clearing was a chestnut tree with low branches. Cassie followed the

other cinema-goers as they ducked under.
Roxy was next, then Alex.

Suddenly, Cassie heard Roxy cry out,
'Oh no!'

She turned round and saw that a branch
had snagged Roxy's cap, letting her black

hair tumble free. As Cassie and Alex rushed to help Roxy, her sunglasses also slipped off.

'Look!' cried a girl. 'It's Roxy Gold!'

'Hey, Roxy!' her friend called. 'Can I have your autograph?'

'Me too!' said a woman.

Roxy put her hat and glasses back on but it was too late – a queue of fans was already forming behind her. Everyone wanted Roxy's autograph!

Roxy sighed. 'I wish sometimes that no one would notice me,' she told Cassie.

Cassie's bracelet jangled, reminding her of something Stella had said. What was it? 'Sometimes people don't want to be in the spotlight . . .'

Hmm, she thought. *Roxy's so famous that it's as if she's always in the spotlight. But she doesn't want people to see her . . .*

Suddenly, Cassie took Alex's arm and led him away from the crowd. Comet bounded after them.

'I think I know what kind of magic my cupcake charm gives me,' Cassie said. 'I think it has the power to make me invisible!'

'Really?' he said. 'Then you *could* make Roxy invisible!'

Cassie shook her head. 'No. That would give away my secret. You're the only other person to know about it, and that's the way it's got to stay.'

'Why don't you experiment with the charm?' Alex suggested.

76

'Good idea,' said Cassie.

They squeezed back through the crowd.
Roxy was still signing autographs and
posing for pictures, but her smile didn't
make her eyes sparkle. *I need to put my plan
into action*, Cassie thought.

'Roxy, would you look after Comet for

a moment, please?' Cassie asked. 'We'll be
back soon.'

'Sure,' said Roxy,
taking Comet's lead
and giving the
little puppy a
cuddle. 'Shame
you can't sign
your pawprint,
Comet.'

Cassie led
Alex behind
an enormous
oak tree. It
had a thick
trunk and lots of branches that hid them
from the clearing. She gripped his hand

and concentrated on her butterfly charm. Instantly, everyone and everything around them was still and silent. Cassie peered around the tree at Roxy and Comet, who were frozen to the spot. The crowd around them was frozen to the spot too.

'You've stopped time!' Alex said excitedly.

Cassie nodded. 'Now we've got a while to try out my new charm,' she said.

Cassie let go of his hand and concentrated on her cupcake charm. Silvery sparkles swirled around it. They danced in the air then drifted to her fingertips and along her arm.

Alex gasped. 'Your hand's disappeared! Your arm's fading now!'

Cassie tingled all over as
sparkles spun around her.

'I don't believe it!'
Alex breathed. 'You're
invisible!'

Cassie touched
Alex's arm.
Sparkles
streamed all
around him
too.

'Wow!' he
said. 'Now I'm invisible!'

Cassie giggled. 'I can hear you, but I
can't see you.'

Alex laughed in delight, then said, 'Let's
hold hands in case we lose each other.'

'We'll need both hands free,' said Cassie. 'I've got an idea to distract everyone from poor Roxy – and it'll show us where we both are, as well. First, I'll use my flower charm to make something magical appear.'

She held her wrist up, then gasped.

'My bracelet's invisible too,' she cried. 'I can't see the charm!'

7
Fairies!

'Now what?' came Alex's voice, from beside her left ear.

'Let me think,' said Cassie. 'Hey! That's it – I'll think, really hard. Maybe I don't have to actually *see* the charm for the magic to work.'

Cassie pictured the flower charm in her mind and concentrated. She held her invisible hands out, palm up.

Think, Cassie she told herself.

Her palms tingled and two glowing golden lights appeared before her. She moved her hands, and the lights moved too.

'Did you create those lights?' said Alex. 'That's scientifically impossible.'

'It's magic, not science,' said Cassie. 'Touch my fingertips, but keep your palms up.'

'Where are your fingers?' asked Alex.

'In front of the lights – that's it!' she said, as something brushed her thumb.

She felt Alex touching her fingertips, and concentrated again.

'Whoa!' said Alex as two more golden lights appeared in his hands. 'They feel like fluttering butterflies.'

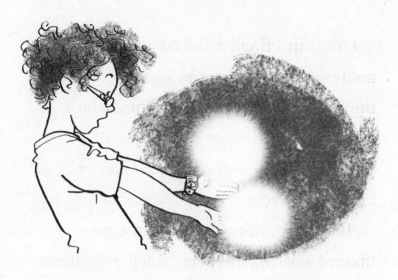

'Fairies, not butterflies,' said Cassie.
'Remember my mum said the Whimsy
Wood fairies looked like little lights? We'll
bring the legend to life! Follow me and do
what I do. Oh!' she said. 'I nearly forgot.'

She closed her eyes and pictured her
butterfly charm. Whirling sparkles appeared.
Instantly, everything and everyone in
Whimsy Wood came to life again. Cassie

saw the crowd around Roxy calling out her name and snapping more photos. Comet licked Roxy, making her laugh as she patiently signed more autographs.

Cassie slipped through the shadowy trees, moving her hands around with the glowing lights. She saw Alex's lights moving nearby. But four tiny lights didn't exactly make Whimsy Wood look filled with fairies.

Just then, Cassie glimpsed something bright over to the left. Another light! And another on the right! And another! Soon the wood seemed full of dancing lights, twinkling like tiny golden stars.

Cassie guessed who had created the lights. 'Thank you, Stella Starkeeper,' she whispered. It really looked as if the legend of Astral-on-Sea was true!

Suddenly, someone shouted, 'Look! Whimsy Wood fairies!'

People called to each other, 'Fairies! Come and see!'

The crowd drifted away from Roxy, and instead followed the dancing lights, gazing in wonder at the magical sight.

Cassie found Alex's hand. She pictured the cupcake charm in her mind. Sparkles swirled, and they could see each other again.

They found Roxy in the clearing, with Comet snuggled in her arms. 'Aren't the fairy lights beautiful?' she said, smiling. 'And look – everyone's gone after them and left me alone!'

'They'll be back soon,' Cassie warned.

The twinkling lights were fading, and people were heading back, chattering excitedly. They'd forgotten all about Roxy.

The Film Star Wish

The three friends settled on a bench.

'By the way, where did you disappear to?' Roxy asked.

'Shh,' said Cassie. 'The film's beginning.' She caught Alex's eye, and winked.

After the film, the three friends set off along the woodland path.

'That was amazing!' said Roxy. 'I've learned lots about Astral-on-Sea, and this is only my first day.'

'It was great,' said Cassie. 'Everyone cheered at the bit about the fairies!'

'What a brilliant idea to have fairies in the wood first,' said Roxy. 'Fantastic special effects!'

Cassie and Alex smiled.

'And they made everyone leave you alone,' said Cassie.

Roxy frowned. 'I shouldn't grumble,' she said. 'I love acting and I won't always be famous. Soon people will find someone or something else more exciting!'

'Like fairies,' Alex giggled. 'But you're so popular,' he added, turning pink, 'you'll be famous for years.'

'I'd love to be famous for a day,' Cassie said. 'It must be so exciting.'

Roxy grinned. 'It is exciting,' she said, 'but it's lovely to have this one afternoon of not being recognized. Now,' she added, 'what disguises shall we wear for Kara's grand opening tomorrow?'

'I might be the astronaut,' said Alex.

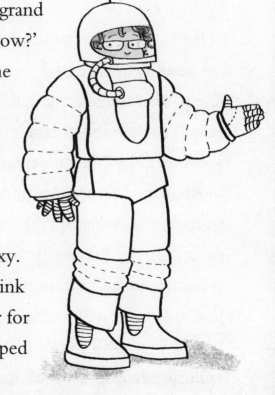

'Shall I be the witch, with a horrid green face?' asked Roxy.

'Yes! And I think I'll be a film star for a day!' Cassie piped up with a grin.

They collapsed into giggles.

'You'll need another disguise for learning to ride my bike,' Cassie told Roxy.

Roxy smiled happily. 'It's going to be a brilliant holiday in Astral-on-Sea!' she said. 'Thanks to you, I can just be . . . me!'

Cassie's wrist tingled. She paused to glance at her bracelet while the others went on ahead. A glittering heart-shaped charm dangled from it, and scarlet sparkles drifted on the breeze.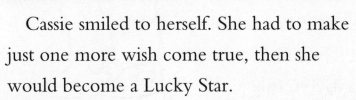

Cassie smiled to herself. She had to make just one more wish come true, then she would become a Lucky Star.

How exciting! But she had a worrying

thought. Alex had been with her through all her magical adventures.

Can I become a Lucky Star before he has to leave Astral-on-Sea?

She hoped so.

Cassie's Things to Make and Do!

Join in the Lucky Stars fun!

The Film Star Wish
Secret Message

There is a secret message hidden on the opposite page. Fill in the letters and discover what it is!

_ _ _ _ _

_ _ _ _

_ _

_ _ _ _ _

Make a Movie

Ever wanted to make a movie? Here's an activity some of the top film-makers use when planning and imagining how their film will look.

Name of film:

....

What type of film is it?

....

(i.e. comedy, cartoon, romance, scary)

Who will star in it?

....

Now you need to storyboard it. This means drawing a picture with a description of each shot in the film. Draw a big version of the template below to describe your film.

1.	2.	3.	4.
Scene 1 . . .	Scene 2 . . .	Scene 3 . . .	Scene 4 . . .
5.	6.	7.	8.
Scene 5 . . .	Scene 6 . . .	Scene 7 . . .	Scene 8 . . .

The Film Star Wish Secret Message

Do you believe in fairies?

Answers

Don't look unless
you're really stuck!

Wishes really do come true

Lucky Stars

The Ballerina Wish

To read an exciting chapter,

please turn the page . . .

1
Crystal Gifts

Cassie looked at Alex's suitcase. It was overflowing with seaside toys, pebbles from the beach and brightly coloured sticks of rock. Alex picked up his microscope and tried to squeeze it in.

'It won't fit,' he groaned.

'Here's one more thing for you to pack,' Cassie said.

She held out a photo album with 'Alex's Holiday' written on the front. For the last

two weeks, Alex and his family had been
staying at Starwatcher Towers, the bed and
breakfast run by Cassie's parents. But now
his holiday was over.

'The album's full of special memories,'
she said, trying to smile.

Alex nodded and cleared his throat. He
smiled back, but Cassie knew he was sad.
Even Comet, his little white puppy, had his
ears down.

Alex opened the photo album and Cassie
pointed to one of the pictures.

'That's the view from Dad's observatory,'
she said. 'You can see the whole of Astral-
on-Sea from there.'

Cassie's dad was an astronomer and
at night he watched the stars from his

observatory. In the daytime, the observatory
gave a spectacular view of the town and the
seaside.

Alex flicked over the page and chuckled.
There was a picture of Twinkle, Cassie's
old tom cat, and Comet chasing a ball.

'They're such good friends,' Cassie said.

'Just like us,' Alex replied. 'I wished for a friend and you became my best friend ever.'

'Your wish was the first one I helped to come true,' Cassie said. 'And you're the only person who knows about my magic charms.'

They looked at Cassie's pretty charm bracelet. Every time she granted someone's wish she received another charm. So far, she had six charms that each gave her a

magical power. The bird meant she could fly, the crescent moon allowed her to talk to animals, the butterfly let her stop time, the flower made things appear and she had the power of invisibility thanks to the cupcake charm.

I still need to find out what power my new heart charm gives me, Cassie thought.

'You only need to get one more charm now,' said Alex. 'Then you'll be a Lucky Star and make wishes come true!'

7

Cassie sighed. 'If only you could stay and help me.'

She blinked away a tear. She couldn't imagine waking up tomorrow and not seeing Alex.

'Thanks for the photo album,' Alex said.

'You're welcome,' Cassie whispered.

Just then Alex's mum popped her head round the bedroom door. She noticed the bulging suitcase.

'I don't think you'll fit anything else in there, Alex,' she said. 'Why don't I pack the microscope?'

Alex showed his mum the photo album.

'That's lovely,' she said. 'Shall I pack this as well?'

'No thanks. I'll carry it on my lap in

the car,' Alex answered.

'Well, we don't
need to leave until this
evening, so you have the
rest of the day here,' his
mum said. She took the
bucket and spade to her guest
room to pack.

'Maybe I can help you earn
your last charm today,' Alex said
to Cassie.

'That would be brilliant!' Cassie
replied.

Alex jigged from foot to foot. 'I've
got something for you too,' he said shyly.

From the wardrobe, Alex lifted out a box
marked 'Top Secret'.

Cassie opened it. Inside were test tubes
filled with beautiful crystals. They twinkled
in shades of green, orange, violet and red.

'Oh, Alex, they
look like stars!' she
exclaimed.

'I grew the crystals
myself,' Alex said
with a grin.

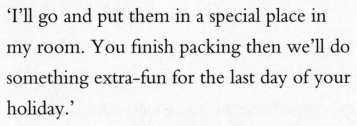

'Thank you so
much,' said Cassie.
'I'll go and put them in a special place in
my room. You finish packing then we'll do
something extra-fun for the last day of your
holiday.'

Carefully, Cassie carried the crystals to
her bedroom. She gave Alex's gift pride of

place on the shelf next to the card she had made for her parents' wedding anniversary. The crystals looked perfect in her room with its glass-panelled ceiling, moon-shaped lamp and starry wallpaper.

Suddenly the crystals lit up, shimmering like a rainbow. Cassie looked through the window. High in the blue sky, zooming between the soft, white clouds, a familiar orb of light was heading straight towards her room.

Rushing to the lever on her bedroom wall, Cassie pulled it down and one of the glass panels in her ceiling swung open. Just in time! The fizzing orb spun in through the gap and landed with an explosion of starlight.

With a *whizz* and a *fizz* and a *zip-zip-zip*, the orb transformed into Stella Starkeeper.

11

Lucky Stars

Her silvery dress shimmered above her glittery leggings and shiny boots.

Cassie gave her friend a big hug. It was Stella who had given her the charm bracelet for her birthday two weeks ago. Now the little charms tinkled quietly.

'You only have to find one more wish to help make come true, and then you'll be a Lucky Star,' Stella said. 'And when you succeed you can grant wishes whenever you please – as long as you feel it's right.'

'Do you think I can do it?' Cassie asked.

Stella's velvety-blue eyes sparkled. 'I believe in you. Remember, I chose you because you like helping people and making them happy.'

Cassie gave a little twirl.

Stella smiled. 'But first you must prove

you are
ready by
earning
your final
charm,' she said.
Cassie nodded.
'I can't wait to
be a Lucky Star,'
she sighed. 'But
I'm so sad that
Alex is leaving.
Look, he gave me
these lovely crystals.'
'They're beautiful,' Stella said. 'Well,
perhaps my clue will cheer you up.' She
touched the little heart-shaped charm on
Cassie's bracelet, making it glow. 'The clue

to the power of this charm is: *memories are precious.*'

Cassie felt a warm glow in her heart.

'And I've got a special surprise for you,' Stella said. 'When you become a Lucky Star, I will grant three wishes you can use just for yourself.'

Cassie's eyes widened. Another wonderful gift!

Sparkles swirled around Stella.

'Don't forget, Cassie,' she said. 'Memories are precious . . .'

And then she was gone, leaving Cassie wondering what the clue meant.

Wishes really do come true

Lucky Stars

Explore the magical world of Lucky Stars!

For fun things to make and do – as well as games and quizzes – go to:

www.luckystarsbooks.co.uk

Wishes really do come true
Lucky Stars

Cassie is training to become a Lucky Star –
someone who can make wishes come true!
Follow her on more exciting adventures as
she meets new friends in need of help.

Find a new magical charm FREE
with every book – collect them all
to become a Lucky Star!

www.luckystarsbooks.co.uk